Hello, Family Members,

Learning to read is one of the most important accomplishments of early childhood. **Hello Reader!** books are designed to help children become skilled readers who like to read. Beginning readers learn to read by remembering frequently used words like "the," "is," and "and"; by using phonics skills to decode new words; and by interpreting picture and text clues. These books provide both the stories children enjoy and the structure they need to read fluently and independently. Here are suggestions for helping your child *before*, *during*, and *after* reading:

Before

- Look at the cover and pictures and have your child predict what the story is about.
- Read the story to your child.
- Encourage your child to chime in with familiar words and phrases.
- Echo read with your child by reading a line first and having your child read it after you do.

During

- Have your child think about a word he or she does not recognize right away. Provide hints such as "Let's see if we know the sounds" and "Have we read other words like this one?"
- Encourage your child to use phonics skills to sound out new words.
- Provide the word for your child when more assistance is needed so that he or she does not struggle and the experience of reading with you is a positive one.
- Encourage your child to have fun by reading with a lot of expression . . . like an actor!

After

- Have your child keep lists of interesting and favorite words.
- Encourage your child to read the books over and over again. Have him or her read to brothers, sisters, grandparents, and even teddy bears. Repeated readings develop confidence in young readers.
- Talk about the stories. Ask and answer questions. Share ideas about the funniest and most interesting characters and events in the stories.

I do hope that you and your child enjoy this book.

—Francie Alexander
Reading Specialist,
Scholastic's Instructional Publishing Group

To Mom, who is always ready
with the soup, toast, and tea
—G.M.

To Edie Weinberg
—B.L.

Library of Congress Cataloging-in-Publication Data
Maccarone, Grace.
I have a cold/by Grace Maccarone; illustrated by Betsy Lewin.
p. cm. — (Hello reader! Level 1)
"Cartwheel books."
Summary: A sick child describes how it feels to have a bad cold.
ISBN 0-590-39638-2
[1. Cold (Disease) —Fiction. 2. Sick—Fiction. 3. Stories in rhyme.]
I. Lewin, Betsy, ill. II. Title. III. Series.
PZ8.3.M1257In 1998
[E]—dc21
98-20284
CIP
AC

10 9 8 7 6 5 0/0 01 02 03

Printed in the U.S.A. 23
First printing, November 1998

I Have a Cold

by Grace Maccarone
Illustrated by Betsy Lewin

Hello Reader! — Level 1

SCHOLASTIC INC.

New York Toronto London Auckland Sydney

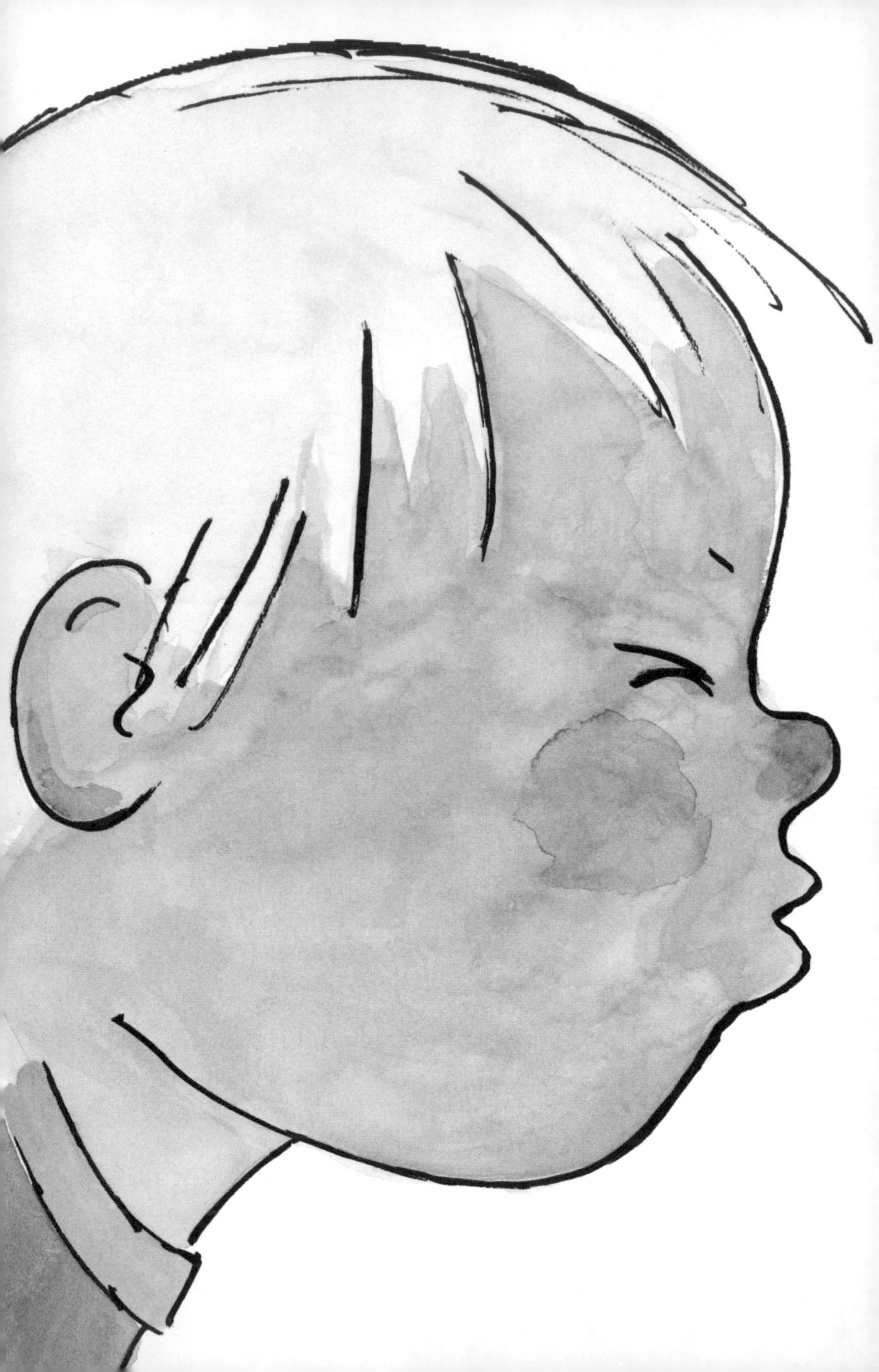

Ah-choo!
Ah-choo!
I sneeze and sneeze.

May I have
a tissue, please?

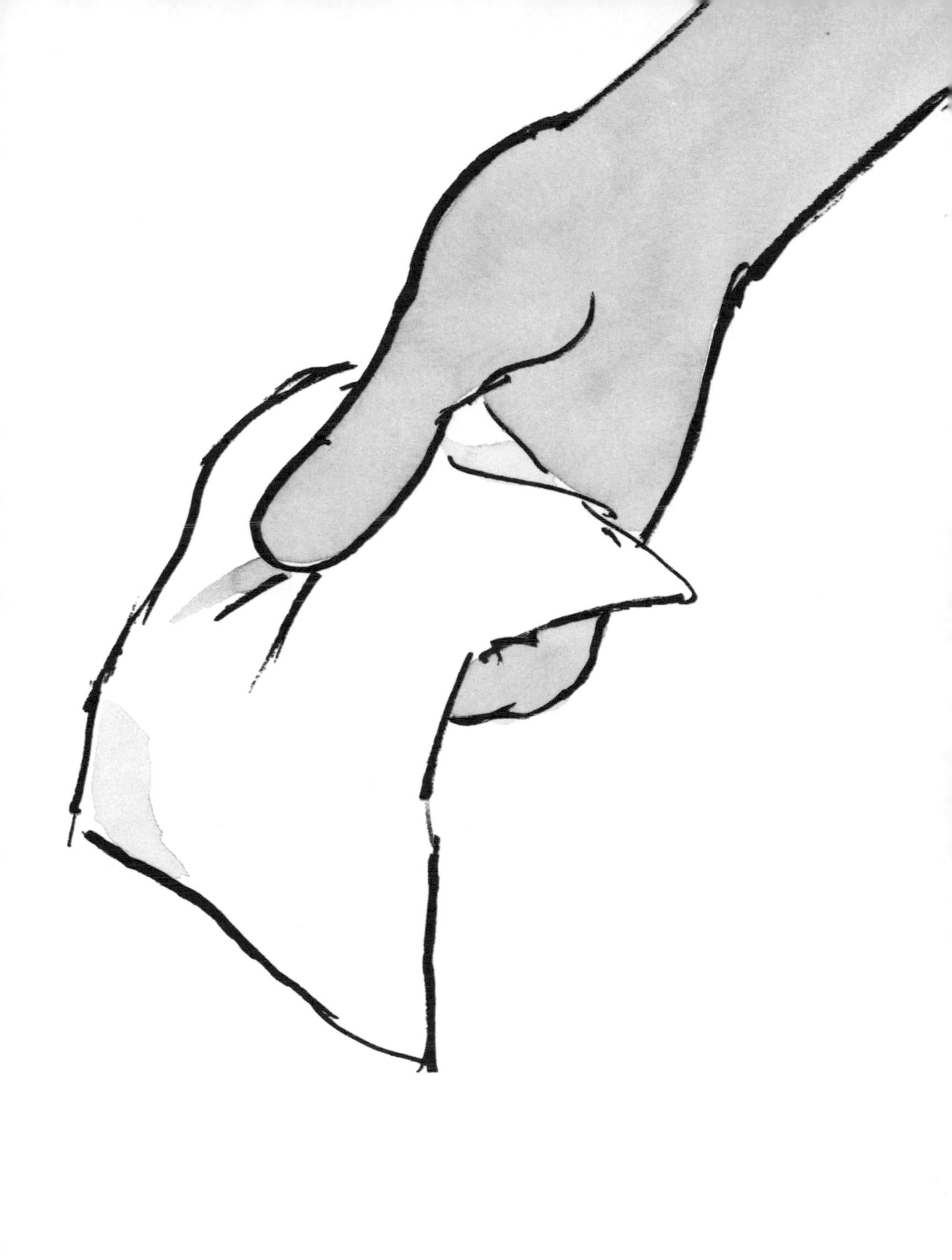

I have a cold.
My ears are stuffy.
My nose is runny.
My eyes are puffy.

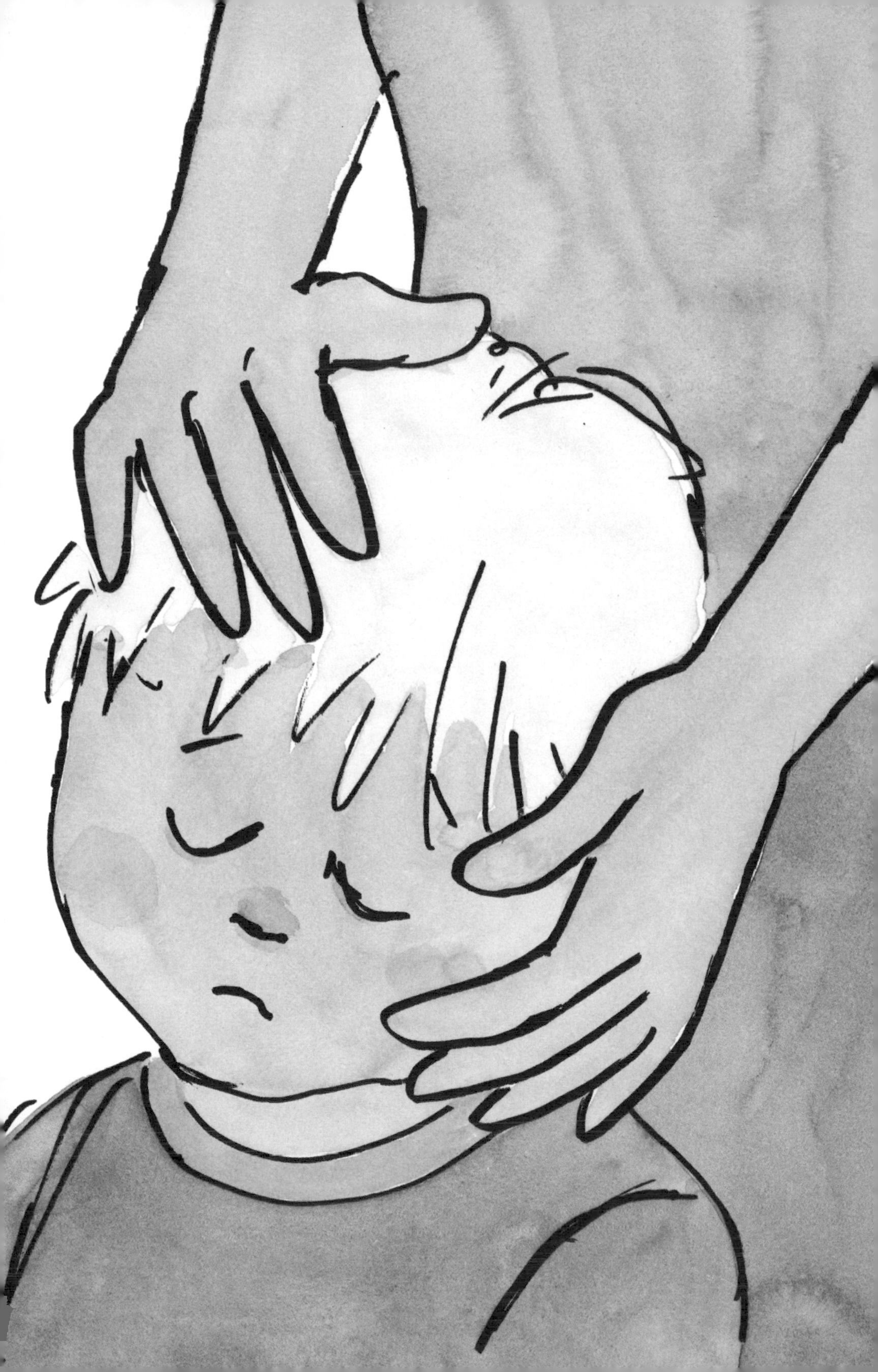

Ah-choo!
Ah-choo!
I sneeze and sneeze.

I blow my nose.
Excuse me, please.

I read a book.

I watch TV.

Mom brings me soup
and toast and tea.

Ah-choo! Ah-choo!
I sneeze and sneeze.

I'm getting sick
of this disease!

My nose is stuffy.
My eyes are red.
I sniffle. I snuffle.
I go to bed.

I make mountains
with my knees.

Dolphins, sharks,
and manatees
swim around
in blanket seas.

Dad gives me
something in a spoon.
He says that
I'll feel better soon.

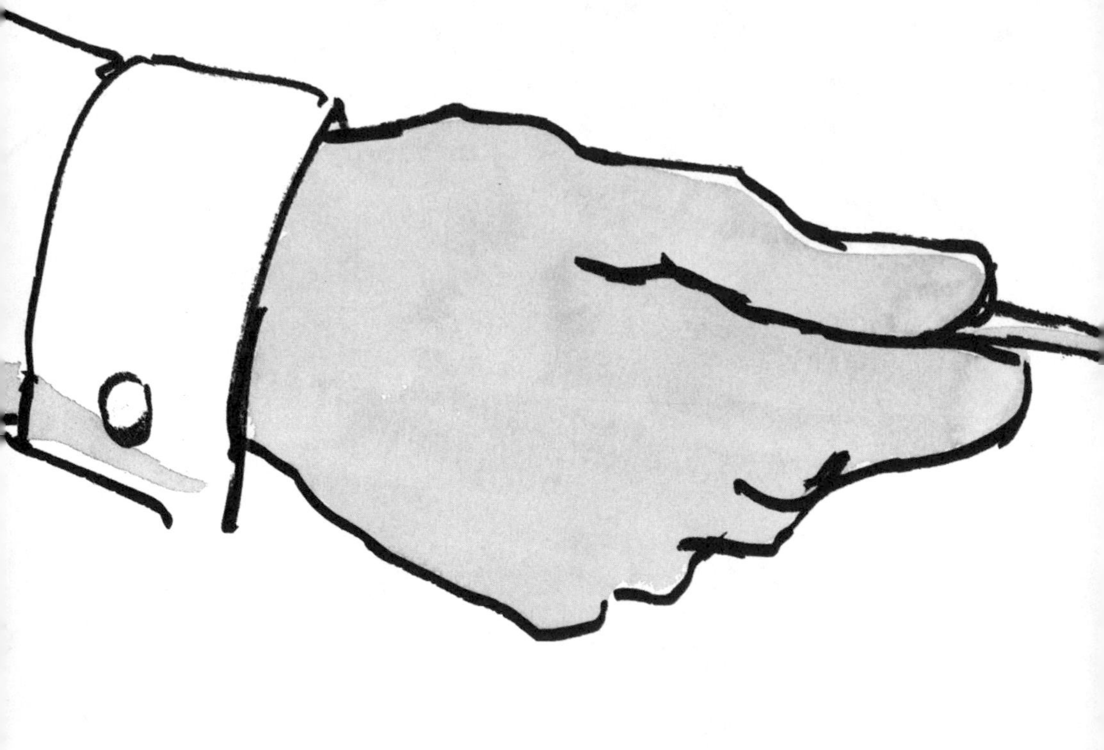

I hold my nose,
and down it goes.

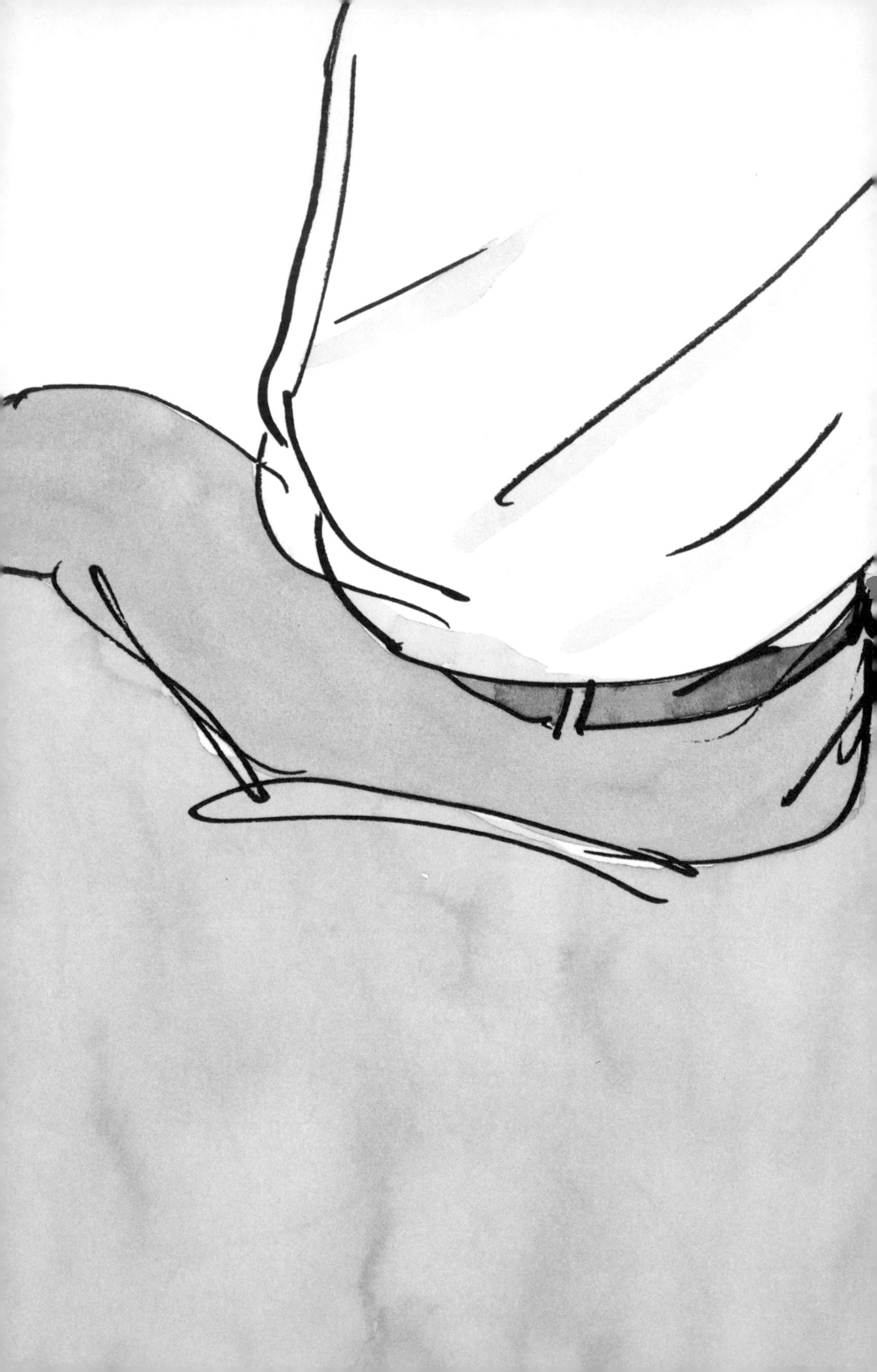

Dad tucks me in,
and then I doze.

Before I fall asleep,
I pray
that my bad cold
will go away.

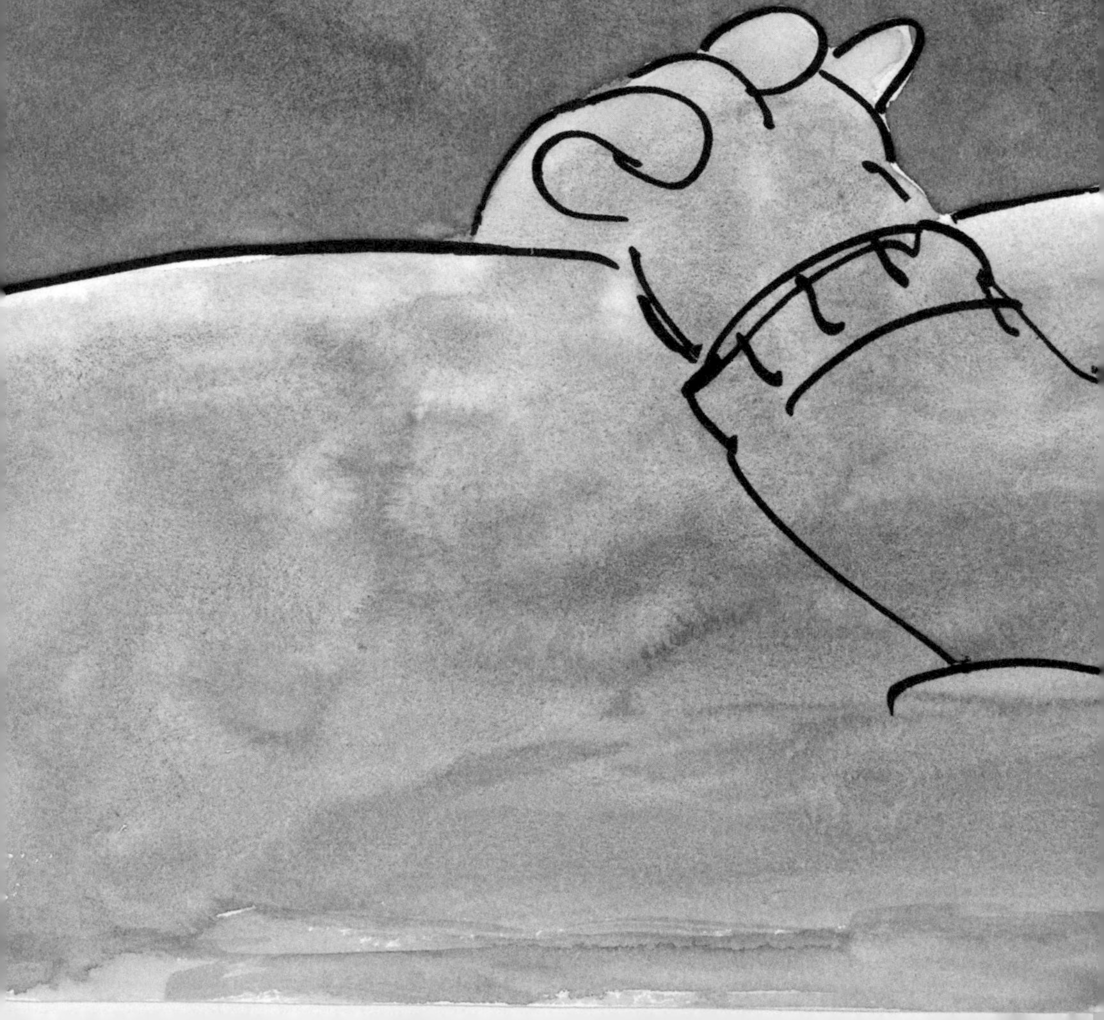

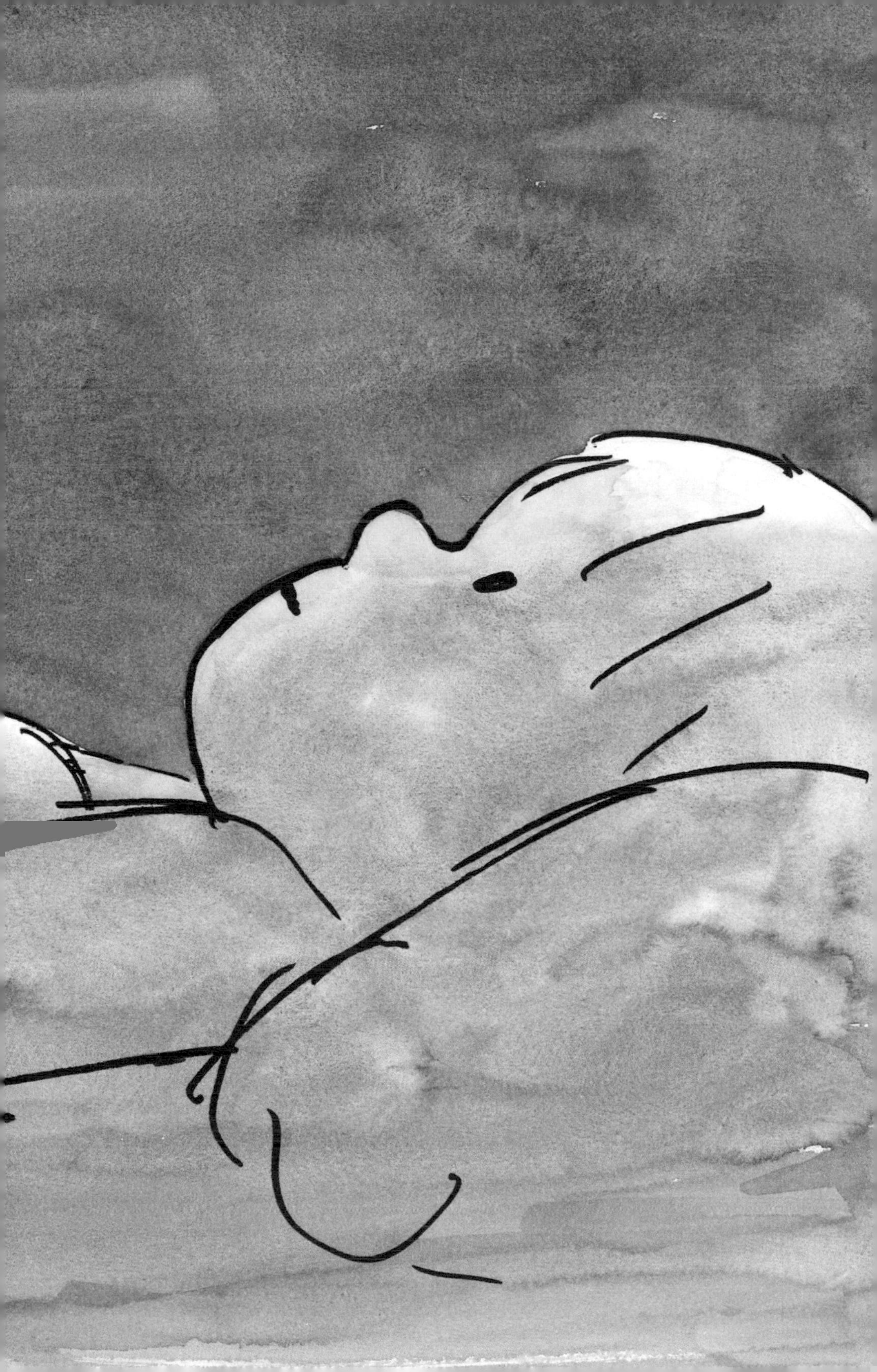

Tomorrow, I'll go out and play!